**PICTURES BY
TOMI UNGERER**

# FLAT STANLEY

## BY JEFF BROWN

HarperCollins*Publishers*

FOR J. C. AND TONY

Breakfast was ready.

"I will go wake up the boys," Mrs. Lambchop said to her husband, George Lambchop. Just then their younger son, Arthur, called from the bedroom he shared with his brother Stanley.

"Hey! Come and look! Hey!"

Mr. and Mrs. Lambchop were both very much in favor of politeness and careful speech. "Hay is for horses, Arthur, not people," Mr. Lambchop said as they entered the bedroom. "Try to remember that."

"Excuse me," Arthur said. "But look!"

He pointed to Stanley's bed. Across it lay the enormous bulletin board that Mr. Lambchop had given the boys a Christmas ago, so that they could pin up pictures and messages and maps. It had fallen, during the night, on top of Stanley.

But Stanley was not hurt. In fact he would still have been sleeping if he had not been woken by his brother's shout.

"What's going on here?" he called out cheerfully from beneath the enormous board.

Mr. and Mrs. Lambchop hurried to lift it from the bed.

"Heavens!" said Mrs. Lambchop.

"Gosh!" said Arthur. "Stanley's flat!"

"As a pancake," said Mr. Lambchop. "Darndest thing I've ever seen."

"Let's all have breakfast," Mrs. Lambchop said. "Then Stanley and I will go see Doctor Dan and hear what he has to say."

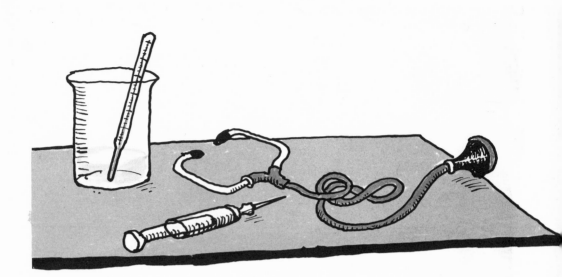

The examination was almost over.

"How do you feel?" Doctor Dan asked. "Does it hurt very much?"

"I felt sort of tickly for a while after I got up," Stanley Lambchop said, "but I feel fine now."

"Well, that's mostly how it is with these cases," said Doctor Dan.

"We'll just have to keep an eye on this young fellow," he said when he had finished the examination. "Sometimes we doctors, despite all our years of training and experience, can only marvel at how little we really know."

Mrs. Lambchop said she thought that Stanley's clothes would have to be altered by the tailor now, so Doctor Dan told his nurse to take Stanley's measurements.

Mrs. Lambchop wrote them down.

Stanley was four feet tall, about a foot wide, and half an inch thick.

When Stanley got used to being flat, he enjoyed it.

He could go in and out of rooms, even when the door was closed, just by lying down and sliding through the crack at the bottom.

Mr. and Mrs. Lambchop said it was silly, but they were quite proud of him.

Arthur got jealous and tried to slide under a door, but he just banged his head.

Being flat could also be helpful, Stanley found.

He was taking a walk with Mrs. Lambchop one afternoon when her favorite ring fell from her finger. The ring rolled across the sidewalk and down between the bars of a grating that covered a dark, deep shaft. Mrs. Lambchop began to cry.

"I have an idea," Stanley said.

He took the laces out of his shoes and an extra pair out of his pocket and tied them all together to make one long lace. Then he tied the end of that to the back of his belt and gave the other end to his mother.

"Lower me," he said, "and I will look for the ring."

"Thank you, Stanley," Mrs. Lambchop said. She lowered him between the bars and moved him carefully up and down and from side to side, so that he could search the whole floor of the shaft.

Two policemen came by and stared at Mrs. Lambchop as she stood holding the long lace that ran down through the grating. She pretended not to notice them.

"What's the matter, lady?" the first policeman asked. "Is your yo-yo stuck?"

"I am not playing with a yo-yo!" Mrs. Lambchop said sharply. "My son is at the other end of this lace, if you must know."

"Get the net, Harry," said the second policeman. "We have caught a cuckoo!"

Just then, down in the shaft, Stanley cried out, "Hooray!"

Mrs. Lambchop pulled him up and saw that he had the ring.

"Good for you, Stanley," she said. Then she turned angrily to the policemen.

"A cuckoo, indeed!" she said. "Shame!"

The policemen apologized. "We didn't get it, lady," they said. "We have been hasty. We see that now."

"People should think twice before making rude remarks," said Mrs. Lambchop. "And then not make them at all."

The policemen realized that was a good rule and said they would try to remember it.

One day Stanley got a letter from his friend Thomas Anthony Jeffrey, whose family had moved recently to California. A school vacation was about to begin and Stanley was invited to spend it with the Jeffreys.

"Oh, boy!" Stanley said. "I would love to go!"

Mr. Lambchop sighed. "A round-trip train or airplane ticket to California is very expensive," he said. "I will have to think of some cheaper way."

When Mr. Lambchop came home from the office that evening, he brought with him an enormous brown-paper envelope.

"Now then, Stanley," he said. "Try this for size."

The envelope fit Stanley very well. There was even room left over, Mrs. Lambchop discovered, for an egg-salad sandwich made with thin bread, and a flat cigarette case filled with milk.

They had to put a great many stamps on the envelope to pay for both airmail and insurance, but it was still much less expensive than a train or airplane ticket to California would have been.

The next day Mr. and Mrs. Lambchop slid Stanley into his envelope, along with the egg-salad sandwich and the cigarette case full of milk, and mailed him from the box on the corner. The envelope had to be folded to fit through the slot, but Stanley was a limber boy and inside the box he straightened right up again.

Mrs. Lambchop was nervous because Stanley had never been away from home alone before. She rapped on the box.

"Can you hear me, dear?" she called. "Are you all right?"

Stanley's voice came quite clearly. "I'm fine. Can I eat my sandwich now?"

"Wait an hour. And try not to get overheated, dear," Mrs. Lambchop said. Then she and Mr. Lambchop cried out "Good-bye, good-bye!" and went home.

Stanley had a fine time in California. When the visit was over, the Jeffreys returned him in a beautiful white envelope they had made themselves. It had red-and-blue markings to show that it was airmail, and Thomas Jeffrey had lettered it "Valuable" and "Fragile" and "This End Up" on both sides.

Back home Stanley told his family that he had been handled so carefully he never felt a single bump. Mr. Lambchop said it proved that jet planes were wonderful, and so was the Post Office Department, and that this was a great age in which to live.

Stanley thought so too.

Mr. Lambchop had always liked to take the boys off with him on Sunday afternoons, to a museum or roller-skating in the park, but it was difficult when they were crossing streets or moving about in crowds. Stanley and Arthur would often be jostled from his side and Mr. Lambchop worried about speeding taxis or that hurrying people might accidentally knock them down.

It was easier after Stanley got flat.

Mr. Lambchop discovered that he could roll Stanley up without hurting him at all. He would tie a piece of string around Stanley to keep him from unrolling and make a little loop in the string for himself. It was as simple as carrying a parcel, and he could hold on to Arthur with the other hand.

Stanley did not mind being carried because he had never much liked to walk. Arthur didn't like to walk either, but he had to. It made him mad.

One Sunday afternoon, in the street, they met an old college friend of Mr. Lambchop's, a man he had not seen for years.

"Well, George, I see you have bought some wallpaper," the man said. "Going to decorate your house, I suppose?"

"Wallpaper?" said Mr. Lambchop. "Oh, no. This is **my** son Stanley."

He undid the string and Stanley unrolled.

"How do you do?" Stanley said.

"Nice to meet you, young feller," the man said. He said to Mr. Lambchop, "George, that boy is flat."

"Smart, too," Mr. Lambchop said. "Stanley is third from the top in his class at school."

"Phooey!" said Arthur.

"This is my younger son, Arthur," Mr. Lambchop said. "And he will apologize for his rudeness."

Arthur could only blush and apologize.

Mr. Lambchop rolled Stanley up again and they set out for home. It rained quite hard while they were on the way. Stanley, of course, hardly got wet at all, just around the edges, but Arthur got soaked.

Late that night Mr. and Mrs. Lambchop heard a noise out in the living room. They found Arthur lying on the floor near the bookcase. He had piled a great many volumes of the *Encyclopaedia Britannica* on top of himself.

"Put some more on me," Arthur said when he saw them. "Don't just stand there. Help me."

Mr. and Mrs. Lambchop sent him back to bed, but the next morning they spoke to Stanley. "Arthur can't help being jealous," they said. "Be nice to him. You're his big brother, after all."

Stanley and Arthur were in the park. The day was sunny, but windy too, and many older boys were flying beautiful, enormous kites with long tails, made in all the colors of the rainbow.

Arthur sighed. "Someday," he said, "I will have a big kite and I will win a kite-flying contest and be famous like everyone else. *Nobody* knows who I am these days."

Stanley remembered what his parents had said. He went to a boy whose kite was broken and borrowed a large spool of string.

"You can fly me, Arthur," he said. "Come on."

He attached the string to himself and gave Arthur the spool to hold. He ran lightly across the grass, sideways to get up speed, and then he turned to meet the breeze.

Up, up, up . . . UP! went Stanley, being a kite.

He knew just how to manage on the gusts of wind. He faced full into the wind if he wanted to rise, and let it take him from behind when he wanted speed. He had only to turn his thin edge to the wind, carefully, a little at a time, so that it did not hold him, and then he would slip gracefully down toward the earth again.

Arthur let out all the string and Stanley soared high above the trees, a beautiful sight, in his green sweater and brown trousers, against the pale-blue sky.

Everyone in the park stood still to watch.

Stanley swooped right and then left in long, matched swoops. He held his arms by his sides and zoomed at the ground like a rocket and curved up again toward the sun. He sideslipped and circled, and made figure eights and crosses and a star.

Nobody has ever flown the way Stanley Lambchop flew that day. Probably no one ever will again.

After a while, of course, people grew tired of watching and Arthur got tired of running about with the empty spool. Stanley went right on though, showing off.

Three boys came up to Arthur and invited him to join them for a hot dog and some soda pop. Arthur left the spool wedged in the fork of a tree. He did not notice, while he was eating the hot dog, that the wind was blowing the string and tangling it about the tree.

The string got shorter and shorter, but Stanley did not realize how low he was until leaves brushed his feet, and then it was too late. He got stuck in the branches. Fifteen minutes passed before Arthur and the other boys heard his cries and climbed up to set him free.

Stanley would not speak to his brother that evening, and at bedtime, even though Arthur had apologized, he was still cross.

Alone with Mr. Lambchop in the living room, Mrs. Lambchop sighed and shook her head. "You're at the office all day, having fun," she said. "You don't realize what I go through with the boys. They're very difficult."

"Kids are like that," Mr. Lambchop said. "Phases. Be patient, dear."

Mr. and Mrs. O. Jay Dart lived in the apartment above the Lambchops. Mr. Dart was an important man, the director of the Famous Museum of Art downtown in the city.

Stanley Lambchop had noticed in the elevator that Mr. Dart, who was ordinarily a cheerful man, had become quite gloomy, but he had no idea what the reason was. And then at breakfast one morning he heard Mr. and Mrs. Lambchop talking about Mr. Dart.

"I see," said Mr. Lambchop, reading the paper over his coffee cup, "that still another painting has been stolen from the Famous Museum. A Toulouse-Lautrec."

Mrs. Lambchop sipped her coffee. "That probably made it easy to steal," she said. "Being too loose, I mean."

"It says," Mr. Lambchop went on, "that Mr. O. Jay Dart, the director, is at his wits' end. The police are no help.

Listen to what the Chief of Police told the newspaper. 'We suspect a gang of sneak thieves. These are the worst kind. They work by sneakery, which makes them very difficult to catch. However, my men and I will keep trying. Meanwhile, I hope people will buy tickets for the Policemen's Ball and not park their cars where signs say don't.' "

The next morning Stanley Lambchop heard Mr. Dart talking to his wife in the elevator.

"These sneak thieves work at night," Mr. Dart said. "It is very hard for our guards to stay awake when they have been on duty all day. And the Famous Museum is so big we cannot guard every picture at the same time. I fear it is hopeless, hopeless, hopeless!"

Suddenly, as if an electric light bulb had lit up in the air above his head, giving out little shooting lines of excitement, Stanley Lambchop had an idea. He told it to Mr. Dart.

"Stanley," Mr. Dart said, "if your mother will give her permission, I will put you and your plan to work this very night!"

Mrs. Lambchop gave her permission. "But you will have to take a long nap this afternoon," she said. "I won't have you up till all hours unless you do."

That evening, after a long nap, Stanley went with Mr. Dart to the Famous Museum. Mr. Dart took him into the main hall, where the biggest and most important paintings were hung. He pointed to a huge painting that showed a bearded man, wearing a floppy velvet hat, playing a violin for a lady who lay on a couch. There was a half-man, half-horse person standing behind them, and three fat children with wings were flying around above. That, Mr. Dart explained, was the most expensive painting in the world!

There was an empty picture frame on the opposite wall. We shall hear more about that later on.

Mr. Dart took Stanley into his office and said, "It is time for you to put on a disguise."

"I already thought of that," Stanley Lambchop said, "and I brought one. My cowboy suit. It has a red bandanna that I can tie over my face. Nobody will recognize me in a million years."

"No," Mr. Dart said. "You will have to wear the disguise I have chosen."

From a closet he took a white dress with a blue sash, a pair of shiny little pointed shoes, a wide straw hat with a blue band that matched the sash, and a wig and a stick. The wig was made of blond hair, long and done in ringlets. The stick was curved at the top and it, too, had a blue ribbon on it.

"In this shepherdess disguise," Mr. Dart said, "you will look like a painting that belongs in the main hall. We do not have cowboy pictures in the main hall."

Stanley was so disgusted he could hardly speak. "I will look like a girl, that's what I will look like," he said. "I wish I had never had my idea."

But he was a good sport, so he put on the disguise.

Back in the main hall Mr. Dart helped Stanley climb up into the empty picture frame. Stanley was able to stay in place because Mr. Dart had cleverly put four small spikes in the wall, one for each hand and foot.

The frame was a perfect fit. Against the wall, Stanley looked just like a picture.

"Except for one thing," Mr. Dart said. "Shepherdesses are supposed to look happy. They smile at their sheep and at the sky. You look fierce, not happy, Stanley."

Stanley tried hard to get a faraway look in his eyes and even to smile a little bit.

Mr. Dart stood back a few feet and stared at him for a moment. "Well," he said, "it may not be art, but I know what I like."

He went off to make sure that certain other parts of Stanley's plan were being taken care of, and Stanley was left alone.

It was very dark in the main hall. A little bit of moonlight came through the windows, and Stanley could just make out the world's most expensive painting on the opposite wall. He felt as though the bearded man with the violin and the lady on the couch and the half-horse person and the winged children were all waiting, as he was, for something to happen.

Time passed and he got tireder and tireder. Anyone would be tired this late at night, especially if he had to stand in a picture frame balancing on little spikes.

Maybe they won't come, Stanley thought. Maybe the sneak thieves won't come at all.

The moon went behind a cloud and then the main hall was pitch dark. It seemed to get quieter, too, with the darkness. There was absolutely no sound at all. Stanley felt the hair on the back of his neck prickle beneath the golden curls of the wig.

*Cr-eee-eee-k* . . .

The creaking sound came from right out in the middle of the main hall and even as he heard it Stanley saw, in the same place, a tiny yellow glow of light!

The creaking came again and the glow got bigger. A trap door had opened in the floor and two men came up through it into the hall!

Stanley understood everything all at once. These must be the sneak thieves! They had a secret trap door entrance into the museum from outside. That was why they had never been caught. And now, tonight, they were back to steal the most expensive painting in the world!

He held very still in his picture frame and listened to the sneak thieves.

"This is it, Max," said the first one. "This is where we art robbers pull a sensational job whilst the civilized community sleeps."

"Right, Luther," said the other man. "In all this great city there is no one to suspicion us."

Ha, ha! thought Stanley Lambchop. That's what you think!

The sneak thieves put down their lantern and took the world's most expensive painting off the wall.

"What would we do to anyone who tried to capture us, Max?" the first man asked.

"We would kill him. What else?" his friend replied.

That was enough to frighten Stanley, and he was even more frightened when Luther came over and stared at him.

"This sheep girl," Luther said. "I thought sheep girls were supposed to smile, Max. This one looks scared."

Just in time, Stanley managed to get a faraway look in his eyes again and to smile, sort of.

"You're crazy, Luther," Max said. "She's smiling. And what a pretty little thing she is, too."

*That* made Stanley furious. He waited until the sneak thieves had turned back to the world's most expensive painting, and then he shouted in his loudest, most terrifying voice: "POLICE! POLICE! MR. DART! THE SNEAK THIEVES ARE HERE!"

The sneak thieves looked at each other. "Max," said the first one, very quietly, "I think I heard the sheep girl yell."

"I think I did too," said Max in a quivery voice. "Oh, boy! Yelling pictures. We both need a rest."

"You'll get a rest, all right!" shouted Mr. Dart, rushing in with the Chief of Police and lots of guards and policemen behind him. "You'll get *ar-rested*, that's what! Ha, ha, ha!"

The sneak thieves were too mixed up by Mr. Dart's joke and too frightened by the policemen to put up a fight. Before they knew it, they had been handcuffed and led away to jail.

The next morning in the office of the Chief of Police Stanley Lambchop got a medal. The day after that his picture was in all the newspapers.

For a while Stanley Lambchop was a famous name. Everywhere that Stanley went, people stared and pointed at him. He could hear them whisper, "Over there, Harriet, over there! That must be Stanley Lambchop, the one who caught the sneak thieves. . . ." and things like that.

But after a few weeks the whispering and the staring stopped. People had other things to think about. Stanley did not mind. Being famous had been fun, but enough was enough.

And then came a further change, and it was not a pleasant one. People began to laugh and make fun of him as he passed by. "Hello, Super-Skinny!" they would shout, and even ruder things, about the way he looked.

Stanley told his parents how he felt. "It's the other kids I mostly mind," he said. "They don't like me any more because I'm different. Flat."

"Shame on them," Mrs. Lambchop said. "It is wrong to dislike people for their shapes. Or their religion, for that matter, or the color of their skin."

"I know," Stanley said. "Only maybe it's impossible for everybody to like *everybody*."

"Perhaps," said Mrs. Lambchop. "But they can try."

Later that night Arthur Lambchop was woken by the sound of crying. In the darkness he crept across the room and knelt by Stanley's bed.

"Are you okay?" he said.

"Go away," Stanley said.

"Don't be mad at me," Arthur said. "You're still mad because I let you get tangled the day you were my kite, I guess."

"Skip it, will you?" Stanley said. "I'm not mad. Go away."

"Please let's be friends. . . ." Arthur couldn't help crying a little, too. "Oh, Stanley," he said. "Please tell me what's wrong?"

Stanley waited for a long time before he spoke. "The thing is," he said, "I'm just not happy any more. I'm tired of being flat. I want to be a regular shape again, like other people. But I'll have to go on being flat forever. It makes me sick."

"Oh, Stanley," Arthur said. He dried his tears on a corner of Stanley's sheet and could think of nothing more to say.

"Don't talk about what I just said," Stanley told him. "I don't want the folks to worry. That would only make it worse."

"You're brave," Arthur said. "You really are."

He took hold of Stanley's hand. The two brothers sat together in the darkness, being friends. They were both still sad, but each one felt a *little* better than he had before.

And then, suddenly, though he was not even trying to think, Arthur had an idea. He jumped up and turned on the light and ran to the big storage box where toys and things were kept. He began to rummage in the box.

Stanley sat up in bed to watch.

Arthur flung aside a football and some lead soldiers and airplane models and lots of wooden blocks, and then he said, "Aha!" He had found what he wanted—an old bicycle pump. He held it up, and Stanley and he looked at each other.

"Okay," Stanley said at last. "But take it easy." He put the end of the long pump hose in his mouth and clamped his lips tightly about it so that no air could escape.

"I'll go slowly," Arthur said. "If it hurts or anything, wiggle your hand at me."

He began to pump. At first nothing happened except that Stanley's cheeks bulged a bit. Arthur watched his hand, but there was no wiggle signal, so he pumped on. Then, suddenly, Stanley's top half began to swell.

"It's working! It's working!" shouted Arthur, pumping away.

Stanley spread his arms so that the air could get around inside of him more easily. He got bigger and bigger. The buttons of his pajama top burst off — *Pop! Pop! Pop!* A moment more and he was all rounded out; head and body, arms and legs. But not his right foot. That foot stayed flat.

Arthur stopped pumping. "It's like trying to do the very last bit of those long balloons," he said. "Maybe a shake would help."

Stanley shook his right foot twice, and with a little *whooshing* sound it swelled out to match the left one. There stood Stanley Lambchop as he used to be, as if he had never been flat at all!

"Thank you, Arthur," Stanley said. "Thank you very much."

The brothers were shaking hands when Mr. Lambchop strode into the room with Mrs. Lambchop right behind him. "We heard you!" said Mr. Lambchop. "Up and talking when you ought to be asleep, eh? Shame on—"

"GEORGE!" said Mrs. Lambchop. "Stanley's *round* again!"

"You're right!" said Mr. Lambchop, noticing. "Good for you, Stanley!"

"I'm the one who did it," Arthur said. "I blew him up."

Everyone was terribly excited and happy, of course. Mrs. Lambchop made hot chocolate to celebrate the occasion, and several toasts were drunk to Arthur for his cleverness.

When the little party was over, Mr. and Mrs. Lambchop tucked the boys back into their beds and kissed them, and then they turned out the light. "Good night," they said.

"Good night," said Stanley and Arthur.

It had been a long and tiring day. Very soon all the Lambchops were asleep.

## THE END